The Dancing Dragon

Written by
Marcia Vaughan

Illustrated by
Stanley Wong Hoo Foon

We clean the house and sweep the floor.
We tie strings of firecrackers outside our store.

It's Chinese New Year. There's lots to do.
We hang up red scrolls and paper lanterns, too.

We bake New Year's cakes, sing New Year's songs .
We clang the cymbals and bang the gongs!

I join my friends and all of my kin,
For the New Year's parade is about to begin.

Boom! Snap! Pop! Firecrackers explode
As the lion dancers charge up the road.

Along the street they roar and play,
The loud noise chasing bad luck away.

They spin and growl, they jump and shout.
The lion dancers leap and whirl about.

Now people with flags and banners pass.
Some wear costumes, some wear masks.